Thomas Nelson and Sons Ltd
Nelson House Mayfield Road
Walton-on-Thames Surrey
KT12 5PL UK

51 York Place
Edinburgh
EH1 3JD UK

Thomas Nelson (Hong Kong) Ltd
Toppan Building 10/F
22A Westlands Road
Quarry Bay Hong Kong

Thomas Nelson Australia
102 Dodds Street
South Melbourne
Victoria 3205
Australia

Nelson Canada
1120 Birchmount Road
Scarborough Ontario
M1K 5G4   Canada

© Templar Publishing Ltd 1985
First published by Hamlyn Publishing 1985
Second and subsequent impressions published by Thomas Nelson & Sons Ltd from 1989

Letterland was devised by Lyn Wendon and is part of
the *Pictogram* system © Lyn Wendon 1973-1986

ISBN 0-17-410152-X
NPN 98

Printed in Italy

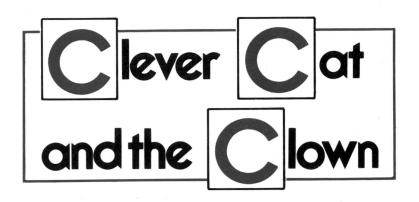

Clever Cat and the Clown

Written by Richard Carlisle
Illustrated by Jane Launchbury

Nelson

Clever Cat was feeling cosy. Curled up on a cushion in the Letterland castle, she fell asleep and dreamed.

She dreamed of cream cakes. She dreamed of climbing trees. Then she dreamed that she could hear curious noises.

Clever Cat woke up. The noises were still there!
"Wherever are they coming from?" thought Clever Cat. So she went to find out.

O utside in the castle courtyard
it was nearly dark.
Clever Cat looked around,
but she could not see anyone.

"That's curious," she thought.
She crept across the courtyard,
waiting for the noise to come again.

It did. It came from behind some
creepers in a corner of the courtyard.
There behind the creepers Clever Cat
found a clown—a clown who was
crying.

The clown had a tall hat with a crimson bobble on top.
He wore baggy trousers and a baggy shirt with lots of crimson spots on it.

He even had a crimson nose and lips painted red to make people smile at him…

…except that it's hard to smile at a clown who is crying.

C lever Cat looked up at the clown. The clown looked sadly down. A large teardrop slid from the corner of his eye and rolled down his cheek. Another tear splashed on to Clever Cat's head.

Clever Cat did not like getting wet.

"Come along, come along, Mr Clown," said Clever Cat rather crossly, as she wiped the teardrop from her fur. "Tell me what's wrong and I'll try to put it right."

"Oh dear, oh dear," sniffed the clown, "I'm so confused. I can't remember where I live. I've lost my memory."

"Crumbs," said Clever Cat, "that's careless. But don't cry. I can usually help. That's why everyone calls me Clever Cat."

"First come into the castle and I'll find you something to eat."

L uckily the castle cook was
nowhere to be seen.
So Clever Cat and the clown
helped themselves to cakes and
ice-cream. That made them both feel
a lot better.

Then Clever Cat started to think hard.
"I wonder where a clown would live?"
she said out loud.

"In a castle?" said the clown
hopefully.
    "That's silly," said Clever Cat.
"What about a cave?"
"Too cold," said the clown. "How about
a cottage?"
"Not very likely," said Clever Cat.

"But I must live somewhere," cried the
clown. "Everyone lives somewhere."

They thought and thought until
morning came. Finally Clever Cat
had an idea.
"How about a camp?"
"Maybe..." said the clown.
"Or a caravan?" said Clever Cat.

" That's it!" cried the clown,
jumping up off his chair.
"I live in a caravan camp!
Oh how clever you are, Clever Cat.
How very, very clever! I can remember
everything now."

"We were having a clown contest.
I am the cannonball clown.
So the other clowns shot me over
to the castle to invite the King and
Queen to come and see our show.
But I landed on my head with such
a bump that I couldn't remember
a thing."

And, sure enough, when they looked over the castle wall, they could see a crowd already collecting around the caravans.

People were arriving from all over Letterland. The sound of trumpets filled the air. That meant the King and Queen were coming too.

The show was about to begin!

The Clown was overjoyed at remembering where he lived, so he cartwheeled all the way to the caravans.

Clever Cat was so pleased with her cleverness that she tried a cartwheel too. But she looked rather clumsy.

"Oh well," she thought. "A cat can't be clever at everything."

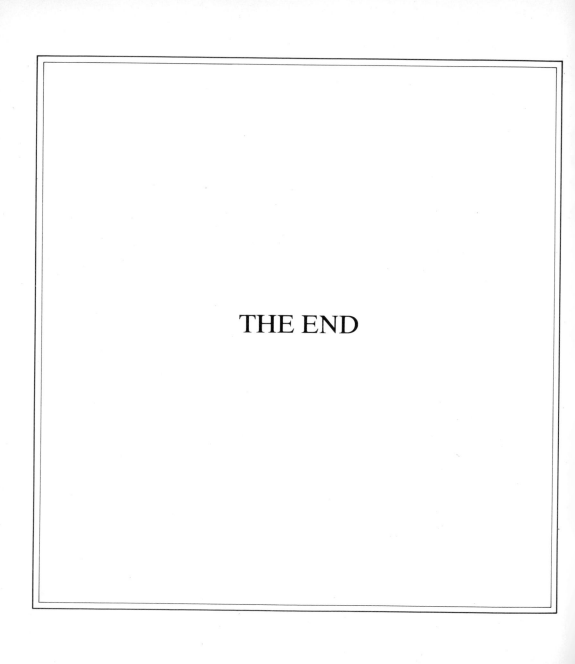

THE END